The Adventures of JIMMY NEUTRON BOY GENIUS

GENIUS 101

Exploring My World

by Jimmy Neutron
as told to Kent Redeker

illustrated by
Mark Marderosian
and Tom LaPadula

Pocket Books/Nickelodeon
London   New York   Sydney

Based on the television series, *The Adventures of Jimmy Neutron, Boy Genius* as seen on Nickelodeon®

POCKET
BOOKS

POCKET BOOKS
First in Great Britain in 2003 by Pocket Books.
An imprint of Simon & Schuster UK Ltd, Africa House, 64-78 Kingsway, London WC2B 6AH.
Originally published in 2003 by Simon & Schuster Children's Publishing Division, New York.

Greetings, everyone! I'm Jimmy Neutron, Retroville's resident inventor and all-around genius. Ever since I built a space fleet out of amusement park rides so my friends and I could do the whole rescuing-our-parents-from-a-giant-alien-chicken thing, people have wanted to know more about me – what I think about, how I invent, what aliens are like – you know, all the basic genius stuff. So I've put all kinds of relevant information in this guide. Should I happen to vanish from this galaxy, people will be able to learn a little about me and my intelligible scientific discoveries.

Table of Contents

YOUNG JIMMY'S INVENTIONS

I have always been busy inventing things – even as a baby. Here's a scrapbook that shows some of my earliest inventions:

Parent Monitor

You never know what kind of trouble your parents might get into if you fail to watch them closely.

Monster Force Field

A baby genius needs a force field to protect him from monsters that sneak out of cupboards at night.

Nappy Dinger

This handy alarm system lets parents know when it's time for changing.

Multiflavoured Dummy

No need to suck on the same flavoured dummy all the time.

Pizza

Milk

Apple

Grapes

Bananas

Peanut

Antigravity Nappies

With Antigravity Nappies nothing is out of reach.

Stroller Coaster

Riding in a stroller all day can get really boring – that's why I invented the Stroller Coaster! Just look at Carl and Sheen playing with bricks – see how boring their lives were before they met me!

MY CYBERNETIC CANINE UNIT: A BOY GENIUS'S BEST FRIEND

Every good inventor needs a faithful lab companion to assist with experiments. However, my parents forbade me to create a cyborg-clone of myself with hydraulic arms and metal teeth. I'm not sure why.

To appease the folks, I decided to create a cybernetic canine unit. I named him Goddard. Goddard has an ultra-lightweight, flea-resistant, titanium body with spring-loaded legs, a telescoping neck and a high-speed computer dome head.

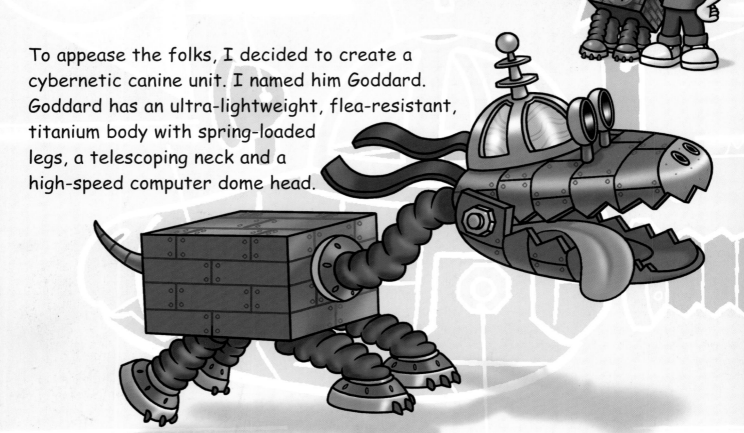

I programmed Goddard to do just about anything, including behaving like a regular (nonrobotic) dog. He loves to fetch, dig for bones and play dead.

These are just a few of Goddard's capabilities:

Lawn Mower

Antilock Brakes

Surfboard

Popcorn Machine

Ping-Pong Table

Lawn Sprinkler

7

THE P-FILES

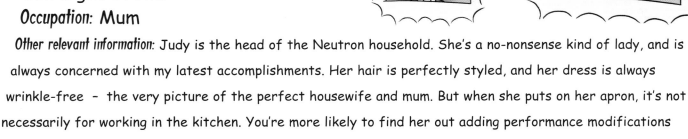

Name: Judy "Mum" Neutron
Height: 5'4"
Weight: Confidential
Eyes: Green
Hair: Light Brown
Occupation: Mum

Other relevant information: Judy is the head of the Neutron household. She's a no-nonsense kind of lady, and is always concerned with my latest accomplishments. Her hair is perfectly styled, and her dress is always wrinkle-free – the very picture of the perfect housewife and mum. But when she puts on her apron, it's not necessarily for working in the kitchen. You're more likely to find her out adding performance modifications to the car than inside baking cookies.

Hobbies: Baking cookies, cutting out supermarket coupons, reconfiguring car engines and solving NASA's emergency technical problems in a pinch.

Secret facts: Judy was a cheerleader at Retroville High School. Some (Carl's mum) say she even had a crush on teen heartthrob Stanley Pomadour. Ewww!

Name: Hugh "Dad" Neutron
Height: 5'11"
Weight: 190 lb
Eyes: Brown
Hair: Thinning
Occupation: Dad

Other relevant information: It appears that I didn't inherit my genius from my dad, Hugh. He is always in a good mood, and usually a little goofy. When it comes to disciplining yours truly, he leaves that up to Mum. He is often as fascinated with my "neato" inventions as I am.

Hobbies: Collects wooden ducks, plays with toy ducks packaged in cereal boxes.

Secret facts: As a teen Hugh listened to really weird music called "New Wave". According to high school friends, Hugh once dreamed of being a manicurist, but flunked out of toenail-clipping class.

One thing I've learned from studying my parents is that when people get older, they sometimes lose the ability to make sense. That's why I invented the Adult Language Translator. Here are some examples of translations from my parents:

Dad says: "Sugar Booger."
Translation: "My wife that I adore."

Mum says: "James Isaac Neutron!"
Translation: "You're in BIG trouble!"

Dad says: "Don't play with big people's fiery flying things, son."
Translation: "Rockets are dangerous."

Mum says: "No more Mrs Nice Mum!"
Translation: "You're in BIG trouble!"

Dad says: "Hey, Jim Jam, let's have a chitchat."
Translation: "I'd like to talk with you."

Dad says: "I've had enough of your inventions for one day, young man!"
Translation: "You're in BIG trouble!"

FAR-OUT FRIENDS

Having good friends is very important – especially if you need practice rearranging human molecules. And I've got two of the best friends!

This is my best friend, Carl. He worries a lot and is really good at sweating. His fondness for llamas is a little weird, but you have to appreciate someone who can win a chocolate-syrup-chugging contest!

This is Sheen, another good friend of mine.

These are the top three things that occupy Sheen's brain:

1. Ultra Lord
2. Ultra Lord
3. Ultra Lord

Sometimes I worry about Sheen. Hopefully his obsession with Ultra Lord is just part of the adolescent experience.

Whenever the three of us are together we always have a blast!

We engage in slime combat.

Once we even played in a band together. We called ourselves the Llama Lords of Science. Catchy, huh?

We also enjoy supersonic sledging!

And best of all, the guys are always ready and willing to help me with my experiments . . . even when they *are* the experiment!

Red Alert: GIRLS WITHIN CLOSE RANGE!

It doesn't take a genius to know that you should avoid girls whenever possible – especially when it's a girl like Cindy "Know-It-All" Vortex!

Reasons to Avoid Girls:

1. They might try to kiss you.

2. They do strange and unusual things to their hair.

3. They like flowers and perfume.

4. They don't appreciate the beauty of a hearty belch.

5. They have nits!!! Although no scientist has ever been able to actually capture and study a nit, there is plenty of evidence to prove their existence.

Here are some symptoms to look for if you have got too close to a girl and fear that you have contracted nits:

1. Drooling.

2. Loss of basic ability to calculate simple thermonuclear physics equations.

3. Acting like a circus orangutan.

4. Uncontrollable urge to skip and hum "Mary Had a Little Lamb".

PUKE!!!

5. Puking.

Unfortunately, despite my best efforts to avoid girls (and their nits), one day an influx of hormones that I can't control will drive me to pursue the female gender against my will.

Work in Progress: THE ANTI-NIT CHAMBER 6000

In preparation for that day, I am currently working on adding a feature to my Anti-Nit Chamber. This handy-dandy addition will remove girl-liking hormones with minimum discomfort.

Nit Spray

Fire Hoses

Mud Bath

Nit Brushes

HOW I GET AROUND TOWN

Now, I *could* take the bus just like anyone. But a boy genius like myself has the brainpower to invent newer and better ways of travelling to school.

Option 1: THE GRAVITY BUBBLE

Bubble travel is the way of the future! Just watch out for trees.

Option 2: PORTABLE BLACK HOLES

If I'm really running late, I can make up for lost time by using my Portable Black Holes.

And if by some fluke of nature they don't work correctly, there is the possibility of landing in some pretty embarrassing places!

Option 3: BACKPACK WITH ROCKET THRUSTERS

My Backpack with Rocket Thrusters always provides an enjoyable ride – and a great view of Retroville!

Option 4: SONIC POGO STICK

There's also my Sonic Pogo Stick. It's great while I'm on it. But once I get off, it takes me a while to stop bouncing.

WORK IN PROGRESS: Some day I hope to be able to travel as a human cannonball!

Unfortunately the crash-test-dummy trials haven't gone too well so far.

The High IQ Inquirer: Inside the Brain of a Whiz Kid

Here's an interview I did for THE HIGH IQ INQUIRER

HIGH IQ INQUIRER: Jimmy, you're obviously an incredible inventor. While still in elementary school you've already invented battery-powered waffles, plastic sharks, and a machine that clones imaginary creatures. How do you think up all of the ideas for your inventions?

JN: Well, I have plenty of time to daydream in class. I mean, we haven't even started studying aerodynamic drag-to-thrust ratios yet!

IQ: Shocking! Our schools have such low standards these days. How many inventions do you think of daily?

JN: I probably think of at least thirty potential invention ideas every day. Like today, I thought of atomic mittens for parrots, grape-flavoured baked beans, and microwaveable calculators.

IQ: Wow! Impressive.

JN: The problem is, I don't have time to actually create everything I think of. So I have to decide which inventions are most worthy.

"I always ask myself, 'Is it cool?'"

IQ: And how exactly do you do that?

JN: Well, the first thing I ask myself is, "Will my invention be useful?"

IQ: Sounds logical.

JN: Yeah, you want to invent something helpful. Something that people will actually use. Like . . . for instance . . . a machine that sucks smog out of the air and turns it into plastic spoons. Ooh! That's a good one! I'm going to write that down.

IQ: I'm watching the Jimmy Neutron creative process in action!

JN: So the smog-spoon machine would be useful. Whereas, a machine that picks fluff out of a belly button, for example, wouldn't be so helpful.

IQ: Did you ever try inventing the belly-button-fluff-picker?

JN: Yeah. But I didn't find it very useful or necessary. That's when I started asking myself the "useful" question.

IQ: What other questions do you ask yourself during this extraordinary brainstorming process?

JN: I always ask myself, "Is it cool?"

IQ: An important question indeed!

JN: Inventing giant robots with laser eyes and car-crushing claws: COOL!

IQ: Definitely cool.

JN: Or inventing a girl-eating plant: also cool.

IQ: Girl-eating?!

JN: You bet! But then, inventing something like a baby doll that wets itself: NOT COOL! That is so *not* cool that even Cindy Vortex might not invent that!

IQ: Who's Cindy Vortex?

JN: Never mind.

IQ: Any other questions you ask yourself?

JN: "Does it go fast?" Any invention that goes really, really fast is a good invention!

IQ: What about "fast food"?

JN: Indeed! I'm working on a supersonic cucumber right now.

IQ: Amazing.

JN: The fourth question I ask myself is, "How long will Mum ground me for when she finds out about my invention?" If she'll ground me for more than two weeks, it's probably not worth it.

IQ: I see.

JN: The last question I ask myself is, "What will the consequences of my invention be?"

IQ: What do you mean?

JN: You have to try and think about what will happen if you construct and use your invention idea. For example, once I tried to cool down a hot summer day by quantumly enhancing some sunblock and shooting it into the atmosphere to block the sun's rays.

IQ: Sounds like a good idea.

JN: Exactly, but it brought on a mini ice age directly above my neighbourhood. It was *really* cold! My mum's hair froze and broke off. And my friend Sheen got his tongue frozen to a flagpole.

IQ: Dear me!

JN: Well, venturing into the unknown is all part of being a boy genius. Now if you'll excuse me, I'm off to meet Carl and Sheen at Retroland. See ya!

TOOLING AROUND

Sometimes I think I should have my own inventor's show so that people could see the tools that I use to invent things!

Retro-Wrench: It's pliers, a screwdriver, a clamp, and much more – all rolled into one

Duct Tape and Gum: No inventor could get very far without these two sticky substances.

Tongs: For handling plutonium.

Laser Welder: Remember to use safety goggles. (Or just have your robotic dog do all the welding.)

Measuring Tape: A definite necessity when measuring rocket engines. (Also, to check if I've grown at all.)

Hammer: I don't always have time to cut everything to fit exactly, so I just hammer things until they fit together.

Fresh Plate of Cookies: These are helpful in getting Carl to help me. (Plus, even a boy genius likes an occasional snack.)

Mop: Lots of my experiments get quite messy.

Apron: Same reason I have a mop.

Cattle Prod: For those instances when your experiments get out of control.

DON'T BLAB, IT'S MY TOP-SECRET LAB

Welcome to my top-secret lab! This is where I create most of my inventions and experiments.

This experiment is where I'm trying to remove the girly smell from flowers.

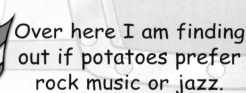

Over here I am finding out if potatoes prefer rock music or jazz.

Or here I'm trying to teach these toasters the alphabet.

This experiment is to determine the effects of sending a trout into the future.

I'm also running an experiment to find the best way to hypnotise my dad, (and then unhypnotise him when I'm through).

EXTRA! EXTRA! EXTRA . . . TERRESTRIALS!

Part of my time in the lab is also spent attempting to contact alien civilisations. Here are some of the alien races that I've already encountered:

YOKIANS: They're green, gooey and kind of mean.

TERROR FISH: They have hovering fish tanks, and they communicate by using bubbles.

BLADDERIONS: Nice guys, but they *always* have to go to the bathroom!

CHOWDERTRONS: These aliens come piping hot! They're peaceful . . . unless you try to dip crackers in them.

BLEEBLES: They come in threes, and are always connected at the head.

GLORF PUDS: They travelled millions of light-years to learn the secret of Earth deodorant.

CINDY VORTEX: I haven't been able to prove she's an alien . . . yet! But she's too creepy and weird to be from Earth.

Meeting alien races may sound like fun, but contacting ETs is not something to be taken lightly! It is important to exercise great caution when attempting to communicate with aliens. In case you've launched your own extraterrestrial communications satellite, I've written up a list of helpful dos and don'ts to use as guidelines.

DO:
- Be polite and list your planet of origin.

- Invite the aliens to a peaceful exchange of knowledge and ideas.

- Have chocolate on hand in case aliens stop by unannounced.

- Have earplugs nearby. Some alien species talk very loudly or communicate in tones that sound like screeching tyres.

- Change your underwear every day. (You don't want to get beamed onto an alien spaceship without clean underwear.)

DON'T:
- Tell an alien race that they look like snot.

- Refer to them as "icky".

- Say that their space suits make them look fat.

- Mention that other alien races consider humans to be "delicious".

- Pick your nose. Most find it really offensive. (Come to think of it, this is a good rule for any situation.)

- Give the coordinates of your planet to an alien race—they might kidnap your parents and sacrifice them to a giant chickenlike monster.

OVER AND OUT

Well that's about it. As you can see, the life of a boy genius can be pretty exciting! I'd like to tell you more about me, but right now I have to go and check on my latest experiment. I'm testing to see what extreme amounts of gamma rays will do to a tiny purple squid. Next time Cindy Vortex tries to use her pool, she's going to get a BIG surprise!

Gotta blast!
Jimmy Neutron